FIGHTING WORDS

BARE KNUCKLE

FIGHTING WORDS

A. S. ACHESON

darbycreek

MINNEAPOLIS

Darby Creek
A division of Lerner Publishing Group, Inc.
241 First Avenue North
Minneapolis, MN 55401 U.S.A.
Website address: www.lernerbooks.com

Cover and interior photographs © iStockphoto.com/Steve Krumenaker (brick
background); © iStockphoto.com/tomograf (paper texture); © iStockphoto.com/
Abomb Industries Design (woodrat); © iStockphoto.com/CSA_Images (fist).

For reading levels and more information, look up this title at
www.lernerbooks.com.

Main body text set in Janson Text LT Std 12/17.
Typeface provided by Linotype AG.

Library of Congress Cataloging-in-Publication Data

The Cataloging-in-Publication Data for *Fighting Words* is on file at the
Library of Congress.
    ISBN: 978–1–4677–1461–7 (LB)
    ISBN: 978–1–4677–2409–8 (EB)

Manufactured in the United States of America
1 – SB – 12/31/13

NEW YORK CITY.
THE 1870s.
THE FIGHT STARTS NOW.

CHAPTER ONE

The jab landed hard on Lester's right side. Lester reared back and struggled to stay on his feet. Myles McReary, his opponent, circled him on the floor of the Woodrat. Lester needed two more hits before he went down, Myles figured. The crowd, split evenly between natives of Manhattan and tourists all the way from Brooklyn, cheered as the teenagers grappled and knocked each other off-balance.

"Get him, you pasty patsy!"

"Lester eats sawdust for dinner!"

"Throw these hoppers back in the river! Show 'em what's what, McReary!"

Lester choked up spit and wiped the sweat off his brow. Lester Wallis. Oakley had told Myles a story about Lester the first day Myles went on the floor. As Oakley explained it, two years ago—back when Lester was the youngest fighter at the Woodrat—he used to tell his opponents, "You're gonna die before me." Now that Myles, seventeen, was squaring off against him, Lester didn't know what to say.

"His eyes, you dog!" a man in the crowd shouted. "Italians can't handle the eyes!"

"Lester Wallis is a Pole, you idiot!" another replied.

"Who cares?" the first man said. "Get him in the eyes!"

Oakley grinned and chewed on a cigar in the corner. Oakley. Myles trusted him, thought he didn't exactly know why. Oakley was rough, and sometimes he wasn't the nicest man in the room, but Myles got the feeling he didn't want his boys to get hurt.

It helped that the Woodrat handed out great payouts for this particular part of the Bowery. Myles knew clubs where they gave fighters IOUs, shooing you out as they told you you'd get payment at the next match. Not at the Woodrat. Oakley and his boss, Lew Mayflower, paid enough for a kid like Myles to get bacon and milk for a week.

"What's wrong, Lessy? Not so bold now?"

"Hey, Myles, what's the matter? Can't hit a boy your own age?"

Quickly, Lester feinted and walloped Myles in the chest. Myles sidestepped left and then right. His right fist, the one Oakley said was a ball of potential, clenched hard as Lester lifted his dukes to his face. Myles jumped back and prepared to give Lester a sidewinder.

Whenever he gave his opponent a sidewinder, the audience cheered, and his opponent fell down. Myles wound up and socked Lester in the stomach. Lester crumpled up like a brown paper bag in the wind.

The Brooklyn fans jeered and threw bottles against the wall. The Manhattan fans went wild.

The room filled up with the tinkle of breaking glass, growing louder as Oakley made his way to the center of the club.

As Oakley counted down from ten, looking down to make sure Lester wasn't planning to get up, a fan on the Brooklyn side hurled a rotten apple in the ring. Oakley looked over at Tracey, watching from behind the bar, and tilted his head. When Oakley got down to three, Tracey picked up the apple thrower and flopped the guy on his shoulder like a towel. The apple thrower kicked and screamed as Tracey went to the door, clearing out spectators and customers along the way.

"Myles McReary is the winner!" Oakley bellowed.

Myles grinned and raised his fists in the air. Half the crowd did the same. The Brooklyn side, disappointed and angry, called Myles so many names he could barely make out what they were. Their voices formed into one big, angry sound—an adult version of what Myles used to hear when his teacher brought up Satan in class.

CHAPTER TWO

"Thirty clams," Oakley said as he counted stacks of bills. "That's the highest I've seen in twenty years, kid. You're a mint."

It was past midnight, and the Woodrat was closed. "A mint?"

"It's an idiom, Myles. It means you make money. You've heard of that building in Washington where government stiffs melt coins?" Oakley waved his hand. "Never mind."

"I suppose that takes care of the rent," Myles said.

"The rent and a lot more. You know what your gift is, Myles? You have the ability to whip up the crowd like nobody else I know. I've seen good fighters, and you're a good fighter too. But it takes a special kind to whip up the crowd like you do."

Tracey wiped off shot glasses with a rag and stooped behind the bar. "The kind who barely says a word?" he said.

"Be serious, Trace," Oakley said. "Myles can build suspense. Kids like him get dewy-eyed barflies hollering as though he's their brother."

"It's a gift, in a way," Tracey said.

"Doesn't feel like it," Myles said.

"It is," Oakley said. "How many fighters have the presence that you have? At most, I can think of three. Maybe two. Just two."

"You and Carly," Tracey said. "If Carly would make an appearance already, we could all retire to Cuba."

"True, but the boys up in Harlem won't let him come down," Oakley said.

"Didn't he sign an agreement?" Tracey said.

Mayflower stormed out of his office. "Did I

hear talk of those uptown rats?" he said.

"You did," Tracey said.

"They burn me behind the ears," said Mayflower. "Pull business from downtown up to Harlem. These days, half the Bowery's itching to make its way up there."

"Who's Carly?" Myles didn't like asking questions like this—they made him feel like he was still fresh off the boat. Most of the time, when he didn't know the answer to a question, he sat and listened until he understood, acting for all the world like the New Yorker he wanted himself to be. Like the real New Yorker his family wanted him to be so badly.

Oakley explained that Carly was a fighter named Giancarlo Sperio. Carly was twenty-three, a few years older than Myles. He was a star in his part of the city. He'd grown up in Yorkville, way up in the ninetieth blocks of the Upper East Side. Everyone who saw him said his skill on the floor was hair-raising.

Local legend had it that Big Benny, for a while the best fighter this side of the Mississippi, went down in a fight against Carly in thirty seconds flat. Spectators came in from every-where—even from Connecticut—to see Carly take down a foolish contender for themselves. If by some magic Oakley found a way to get Carly in the Woodrat, it might well become the most popular club in the city.

"The money at stake is tremendous," Oakley said. "Imagine: customers from Boston, from Philly, from Baltimore. They want to catch a fight, and where do they go? The Woodrat. They ask your well-schooled man on the street where to go, and what does he say?"

"The Bronx?" Tracey said.

"Quit your jokes," Oakley said. "Carly is the key to a fortune. Think of how we could fix up this place if he appeared for just one night."

"What do you mean by *we*?" Tracey said.

"New lamps," Mayflower said. "We could purchase lamps that don't burn out every night."

Myles looked around at the gas lamps dotting the walls. Many, especially those near the entrance, were dim, and one over the door flickered like a broken cable. Even so, Myles thought the Woodrat was perfectly fine as it was.

He thought of Oakley's dream of money, money Myles didn't want to spend on new-fangled toys or fancy lamps for the club. He wanted to send it home, back to his family in Ireland. But he knew that if Oakley and Tracey heard him express such a misty-eyed sentiment, the two would just call him yet another sensitive Irishman. More than anything else in New York, Myles wanted their respect, and to get it, he was happy to look around, to nod and say yes, of course, new lamps do wonders for us.

"Your payout this week is ten dollars," Oakley said as he handed Myles his cash. "A good sum. Now get out of here and go buy yourself a treat."

CHAPTER THREE

Late on Monday evenings, when the rest of his parish was tucked away in bed, Myles paid a visit to St. Anthony's Church on the corner of West Broadway and Bleecker Street. He preferred to pray alone. During his first week in the States, he went to his parish priest, and Father Wiley gave him a key that allowed him to come in as he pleased. Tonight he was hungry, as hungry as he always was after a fight, but not so hungry that he didn't want to get a word in with the

Lord before he got food. After turning the key and opening St. Anthony's massive front door, Myles eased it shut and walked to a pew up front.

He sat on the hardwood and clasped his hands between his knees. There was a book of psalms on the shelf in front of him, which Myles took out and spread open on his lap. Moonlight streamed through a trio of stained-glass windows, lighting up the pages of the psalm book as Myles flipped through. He recited the *Our Father* in Latin, English, and Irish, afraid that he was mangling the Latin and Irish versions. When he was young, his mother used to tell him that God forgets you once you forget the *Our Father*.

He went through the Irish again, to be sure: *Ar nathair, ata ar neamh.* Then the Latin: *Pater noster, qui es in caelum. Our father, who art in heaven.* The high ceilings echoed his words. Myles worried that the glass in the room, the goblets and chalices and bowls, might vibrate and crack if he ever raised his voice.

He tried to find psalms that prayed for health and healing.

My flesh and my heart faileth, but God is the strength of my heart.

O Lord, heal me, for my bones are vexed.

I will triumph in the works of thy hands.

A girl named Grainne taught him these psalms the day after he lost his first fight. Grainne lived down the street from the McRearys. When Myles had appeared in her window one day with a bloody nose and puffy skin, she invited him in to her living room. There, he listened as she recited the few psalms she knew from memory.

Myles had tried to burn the psalms into his mind that day, but after a week of daily recitations, he began to forget certain words. Every time he forgot something, it felt like he was spitting on Grainne. To make up for the forgetfulness, he checked the book every time, aware that his memory was nothing compared to the Scriptures.

He pulled out a drawing of his family from his pocket. On the back of the drawing, he'd written a tally of his earnings thus far. In the corner, he'd also noted the amount of money he needed to bring them over. Three hundred dollars. He scribbled Oakley's payout at the bottom of a long column of numbers. Forty more dollars and he could stop fighting for good.

He didn't like fighting—he never had. Fighting was just something he was good at. He dreamed of a day when he didn't have to ask the Lord to keep him safe. He felt guilty about that dream, though. He knew that when you started to think those thoughts, that was the devil whispering temptation in your ear.

The knob on the front door jiggled. Myles crouched in his pew. There were bruises on his face and arms, and he knew that if a priest came in, he might have to confess his involvement in bareknuckle boxing. If that happened, the word of the Lord might keep Myles out of the Woodrat. But if Myles feared the Lord, he also feared what might happen to his family if he didn't get forty more dollars.

They had never made a lot of money. And from what he could tell from the letters his mother sent over, the carpentry business that kept his family afloat for generations was going under. His father built homes. His grandfather had built homes before that. But these days, the people weren't buying. The family needed all the help they could get. They needed it even if that meant their son hurting God's own children.

Myles's father had never liked boxing. What the man liked were men who stood up for themselves when they had to. Or who stood up for the people he loved.

Myles remembered his father standing up to their landlord. Myles had been seven years old. On a rainy day in February, the landlord appeared at the door with two policemen, who threatened to evict the McReary family with rifles and batons. Myles wanted his father to throw up his hands, but instead, his father rooted himself to the ground, informing the landlord in no uncertain terms that now was the time for him to leave. The policemen raised their batons, but at the last minute, the landlord called them off, giving McReary one extra month to drum up the paltry rent. A week later, Myles's father went to the landlord and gave him two slips of paper:

the rent and a handwritten warning to never bring the cops around again.

The knob jiggled a second time. Myles snuck out of the pew and left the room through a tiny side door, behind which he saw a set of musty stairs. He went down the stairs and found himself in a cellar. A series of grimy windows lined the top quarter of the wall. Back in the church, someone called out, "Who's there?"

Myles unlatched a window and wriggled onto the street.

CHAPTER FOUR

About a week later, Myles sat alone at a table in the Woodrat, working his way through a penny novel he'd purchased the day before. His favorite stories took place on cruise liners or passenger trains. That included *All Clear to Tempe*, the book he was reading now. In this story, a bandit kidnapped a young heiress and stashed her away on a train chugging over the desert. The conductor overhears the bandit on a visit to the dining car and orders his deputy to save the heiress in his stead. As the train moves over the Arizona badlands, the deputy fights to keep the girl from getting hurt.

The engine and its painful chugging struck misery into Henry's heart. A peaceful boy by nature, the kind of man who never stood up for a fight, he barely believed there were men out there who could take little girls from their daddies. The heat rose dreadfully as the raging coal-fire licked at his face and neck . . .

At the bar, Tracey listened to Edward Tower, a cop running through his arrests.

"The fact is these rascals are slum rats. They barely understand what they steal. They pinch and they swipe and they hoard their treasure. But they never spend it in a way you and I would recognize. Did I tell you what happened to me on Monday?"

"No," Tracey said.

"You know the man who runs the fruit stand on 2nd Avenue?" Tower asked. "Obadiah? He calls me last week, and when I get there, he tells me his bananas are missing. I write it down and go back to my business. The next day, his apples go missing. Then his grapes, then his tomatoes, and pretty soon everything's gone. I tell Obadiah, I know this type of menace. I saw it last August on 8th."

"So many scalawag kids these days," said a man at the end of the bar.

"I tell him every fruit stand this side of 14th Street is plagued. I get my deputy to wait outside and catch the criminal in action. Near four, the rat comes by and waits till Obadiah is engaged. He stuffs bananas in his pants, and my deputy cuffs him. When I meet him, I tell him, take me to your home. I want to see the mother that raised you to do this."

"A bit harsh," Tracey said.

"He takes me back to his garbage heap of a tenement," Tower said. "Rotting fruit everywhere. Flies are feasting on pungent apples in the corner. From what I could tell, this crook was taking things yet refusing to eat them. He just wanted to steal, it seems."

Myles tried to block the men out and concentrate on his book:

The rows of prickly cacti implored Henry through the windows. Save this innocent girl! they told him. Henry's mind was aflame and his eyes reeled with visions. He shook with the rage of justice. Grasping a poker from the hot bed of coals, he noted its bright tip was radiating deadly warmth . . .

Tracey had a theory. "Perhaps he wanted to start up his own fruit stand."

"You're a card," Tower said.

Myles dog-eared his book and set it down on the table. As he did, Oakley stepped through the entrance to the Woodrat, grinning like a six-year-old on Christmas morning.

"Patrons!" he said, sweeping through the crowd like a winning candidate for mayor. "As of now, sarsaparilla and snacks are half off in the Woodrat. Pick up a bottle and bring one home to your kids."

"Hey, hey," Tracey said, calling to Oakley across the club. "What will Lew say?"

"He won't mind when he hears my news," Oakley said while approaching the bar. "I just procured us a ticket to health and wealth. Come

June, you'll thank me for the work I did this morning."

The men in the club went quiet to hear his announcement. Myles quickly tucked his novel in his satchel.

"Myles!" Oakley said. "What better man could I ask to see on this day?"

"Am I supposed to answer that question?" Myles said.

Oakley didn't reply. He cleared an empty space for himself on the bar. After clambering onto a stool, he stepped on the slippery surface. He glanced to Tracey and nodded at the door, which Tracey shut and bolted. When the lock was secure, he nodded to Oakley and crossed his arms.

"A week from now, the Woodrat will host the greatest fight in New York history," Oakley said. "Giancarlo Sperio—a man you may know as Carly—will appear on this floor for a once-in-a-lifetime event!"

"Sweet God," said a man near the bathroom.

"How in Joseph's name did you manage to pull that off?" said a man nursing a tonic.

Oakley smiled. "Suffice it to say a certain club in Harlem will be getting a little something in return. As for betting, you boys are free to lay down your greenbacks now."

The screech of shifting chairs filled the club. Half the patrons moved to the bar. As Myles watched, men he knew as his audience during fights passed by on their way to put money on Carly's triumph. Oakley saw Myles and took a seat at his table.

"Hear that, Myles?" Oakley said. "Are you ready?"

"For what?"

"The fight," Oakley said. "The match is you versus Carly. Did you think I'd send in some kind of stumbling greenhorn?"

Myles felt his vision go blurry—light from the nearest lamp clouded his eyes. He closed his fist around his glass of seltzer and struggled not to break it into pieces.

"Might want to get some bandages for the fight," Tracey said.

CHAPTER FIVE

The following Monday, Tracey brought Myles two hundred blocks uptown to get a glimpse of Carly in action. Though Myles had been in New York for close to three years, he'd never once ventured north of the boundary of 14th Street. As they rode a horse-drawn carriage up Broadway, he peered out the window at dense crowds of people and new, disorienting neighborhoods. He sat beside a friend of Tracey's named Anthony, a squat man with patchy hair on his lip. Like Carly, Anthony spoke Sicilian.

"Carly's a foul-mouthed scoundrel if ever I heard one," said Anthony. "Not on the floor. In person. In a fight, he barely opens his mouth."

Outside on the street, vendors called out the prices for handmade wares. Grime-covered paperboys waved copies of that day's *New York Times*. Myles tried to figure out how many people out there on the street were thieves. Tower's tale about the fruit stand made Myles wonder.

Growing up, he had known boys who swiped loaves of bread and the like, but he'd never known boys who stole because they wanted to steal. The notion was strange to him, risking a jail sentence to make life more difficult for a person you barely knew. Myles feared the police in Manhattan, especially those with a bad eye out for the Irish. But when he thought of a cop nabbing one of those men, he felt that justice was at work in the world, somehow.

The carriage passed by the southwestern corner of Central Park. Myles could just see over the top of the gate. In a distant treetop, a boy with frayed shoes and soot on his face looked out solemnly on the road. Myles waved. The boy didn't see him. Tracey and Anthony chuckled.

"You look like a man trying to get out of a cell," Tracey said.

"Do not worry, Myles, I feel the same way," Anthony said. "These things are bad for the soul. Man shouldn't be trapped in a rickety box."

The carriage moved through the Upper West Side and passed by the gate to Columbia University. Looking in through the gate, Myles took in the crowds of professors and students in well-kept coats. An elderly woman sold notebooks out of a cart beside a shoeshine booth. Scholars from all over the country hurried on red brick paths. Watching them, Myles wondered how many of the rich and powerful men in the city had begun their lives as poor as he was.

How did a fighter become a scholar? Was it even possible? Did boys who spent time in seedy clubs ever hit it big in New York? A dapper man idly checked his pocket watch. Myles decided there was simply no way that man was once like him.

Certain men were born in nice coats, he said to himself.

The carriage driver asked Tracey if he knew how to get them to the club. Tracey gave the driver complicated directions. The Harlem club was famous, but there was always a chance—as Tracey had mentioned before they left the Woodrat—that a driver might act as though he'd never heard of it before. Anthony told the driver the club was across from a butcher, and the driver lit up.

"A-ha!" the man said. "The bacon loin there is a gift from God himself."

They pulled up at the club five minutes later. Tracey dropped a sack of coins in the driver's upturned hand. On the street, a band of unruly boys took turns diving into hay piles. Before they pushed open the club's heavy doors. Tracey grabbed Myles and whispered gruffly in his ear.

"Remember what you see today," he told him. "Pay attention to his moves. Stamp them onto your brain."

The fight was halfway done by the time they got there. Carly's opponent, a skinny man with an eye patch and arms that looked like oak branches, flailed with every punch. It looked to Myles as though the man's hands were too heavy to control how far they swung.

Carly himself was spry as a Brooklyn squirrel. He pelted the one-eyed man with dozens of tiny jabs. His jet-black forelock mopped his sweaty brow as he moved about the ring. Near Carly's armpit, a scar the length of a candlestick wrapped from his chest to his back. He raised his fists to guard against the one-eyed man's attacks. The puffy skin on his scar stretched taut over the wound.

On every side, men from all over the neighborhood cheered and called them names.

"Sewer rat!"

"Pig licker!"

"Think I struck oil somewhere in Carly's hair!"

Myles could see that Carly's opponent was close to reaching his limit. His legs were slow, his movement sluggish, his punches wild and sloppy. Myles guessed that the secret to Carly's success was his knack for exhausting his opponents. If that were the case, then Myles was lucky. Oakley once called him by the nickname the Tireless Terror.

"Here it comes," Anthony said. Before the word *comes* had left Anthony's mouth, Carly swiveled and twisted his torso like a pretzel. He released the tension in his fist in one killer blow, delivered with astonishing force at the bottom of the one-eyed man's rib cage.

His opponent crumpled. The audience whooped and sprayed Carly with a bottle of champagne. As Carly raised his fists in triumph, Tracey leaned over and asked Myles what he remembered.

"I remember it all," Myles said.

CHAPTER SIX

Later that night, after Tracey and Anthony had dropped him off in the Bowery, Myles went back to his favorite spot in the church. On the ride back down, Tracey had asked Myles to talk about Carly. He had prodded Myles about the moves that made Carly the fighter he was. Myles had mentioned Carly's strengths, like his side-to-side movements, quick wrists, and impenetrable guard, but his mind was elsewhere the whole time. In the church, he could ask the Lord for the guidance he needed. Only the Lord understood why he was feeling so scared.

"My Lord, *O Domini*, please listen," Myles said. He asked the Lord to think back to when Myles was eight years old. On a rainy day in October, Myles had come home from school to find three boys, all about his age, waiting for him at his front door. They knew him, but he didn't know them—all three were brothers of a girl who Myles had shoved in a ditch a week before. Pinning him down on the ground, they pummeled his rain-soaked body until he blacked out on the grass. When he woke, he had a black eye, bruises, and a broken rib.

The injuries had kept Myles stuck in his house for a month while his body recovered. Ever since that day, his bottom left rib ached, a reminder that at least one part of him couldn't stand up to a punch. In a fight, he did a pretty good job of guarding his ribs, but if Carly pounded him with a blow like the one that took down the one-eyed man, Myles knew it was over for him and his fragile bones. And that would mean the end of his income—the end of money going into the tally in his pocket.

His rib felt tender when he pressed it with his finger. He tried to remember the psalms, but then he realized that what he was asking for was much more than health and healing. He needed the kind of protection the Lord once gave David. For that, Myles needed his own prayer, a prayer that showed God his devotion to his word was complete.

"Lord," he said, clasping his hands in his lap. "Lord and savior. I ask you to hear me on this darkest of darkest nights. I am weak, but I am loyal, and tonight I request your grace."

The knob on the front door jiggled and squeaked. Myles turned his head and waited to see if it would open. It didn't, so he went back to his prayer.

"There is a man, a very strong man, and he will engage me in battle. I hope to fight him well and yet I am hurt. I pray that you will deign to keep me safe as I set forth on my journey—"

A side door opened with a bang. Before Myles could finish his sentence, footsteps echoed through the chamber. He crouched in his pew, hiding the way a small child hides behind a bush, and listened as the footsteps got louder. He crossed the aisle and glanced back. A silver-haired man in a black shirt was strolling leisurely to the altar.

Myles passed through the right-side pew and snuck down the steps to the basement. Underground, he made his way to his favorite window and gently tugged on the latch.

Locked. Myles yanked and yanked, but the metal wouldn't budge. His breathing quickened as the man approached the stairs. When Myles realized he didn't have time to crawl out, he spun around and faced the door. The silver-haired man came down the staircase and halted on the bottom step. He raised an eyebrow.

"Is something the matter?" he said.

CHAPTER SEVEN

Myles rubbed his elbows, a lifelong nervous habit. "No, not at all," he said. "I'm very sorry I broke in."

"You broke in?" the man said. "Did you steal something?"

"No, but I'm not meant to be here."

The man smiled. "Why not?" he said. "This place is a house of God. A Christian may enter whenever the Word compels him."

"Well, I'm sorry all the same, Mister—"

"Father," the man said. "Father O'Carroll. Not 'Mister Father.' I've heard that joke before."

O'Carroll approached Myles. He patted his robe to prove he was carrying no weapons. The two shook hands, and Myles noted the calluses on O'Carroll's palms. They felt like the hands of the men who used card games with his father.

"My name is Myles," he said.

"I'm very glad to meet you," O'Carroll said. "Is that a brogue I hear?"

"What do you mean?"

"Are you from the old country?"

"Which one?" Myles asked.

"*Which one*," O'Carroll said, laughing. "You know very well which one."

Myles told him that he was from Enniscrone, a town with two pubs, one road, and a thousand cows. O'Carroll told Myles that he was from Ballina, a nearby town where Myles used to go to the library.

"A boy who can read is a beautiful thing," O'Carroll said. "Our people have many, thank God, but we need more."

"My father always said it was necessary," Myles said. This was true, though not for the reasons O'Carroll might suppose. Old McReary used to say you couldn't get out if you couldn't read the signs on the road.

"And now you're in New York City," O'Carroll said. "Are you here for fame and fortune?"

"More fortune, though fame would be grand," Myles said. "I'm here to bring the rest of the clan over, you know? I'm here to get a bit in the pocket."

"Saving up for a good cause," O'Carroll said. "Good boy."

"I like to think so."

"Are you a sweeper? They say that Irish boys are the greatest sweepers in the city."

"No." Myles hoped his face wasn't red. "Not exactly."

"Could you be a policeman?" O'Carroll said. "The Irish do well in the city police force, you know."

Should I tell him? Myles thought.

"You could join me in the clergy, of course,"

O'Carroll continued. "I know it's not exciting, but it has great rewards for the soul."

I should tell him, Myles thought.

"I say it's not exciting, but I tell you it's never boring."

"Father, I have something to confess," Myles said. "All is not well. I make my wages from sin."

He then told O'Carroll all about his fighting—about Oakley and the Woodrat—and told him it was not the first thing he wanted to be doing with his life. He told O'Carroll his lawless profession was a means to a noble end. When he got the chance, he wanted to stop, but he worried that Carly would end his career before he could.

"Is God offended that I do such things for the sake of saving my family?" Myles asked. "Does a wrong thing become right if you do it for the health of your people?"

O'Carroll scrunched his brow and considered this messy predicament.

"I prayed for my safety for one more win," Myles said. "After that, I promise to give it up. I promise."

"What makes you think the Lord is unwilling to provide this?"

"Nothing," Myles said. "But I don't know if I deserve it. I wish there were some way for him to tell me I do."

O'Carroll tapped lightly on his pocket. Holding up a finger with one hand, he pointed to where Myles was standing.

"Wait here for a minute," he said.

He turned and went back upstairs. Myles again heard the man's footsteps echo throughout the church. Myles folded one hand on top of the other and rooted himself in place. Was O'Carroll coming back with a punishment? A blessing? Was he coming back at all? He might even leave the church, Myles realized, as a way of showing how the Lord might abandon Myles if he kept up his ways. But a short while later, O'Carroll came back. He kept one hand in his pocket and the other hand clenched in a fist.

"Take this," he said to Myles. He opened his fist to reveal a folded-up strip of paper. Myles took the strip and unfolded it. Inside was written an address on 8th Street.

"By chance are you free tomorrow?" said O'Carroll.

"What time?"

"Early evening. Four or five. Do you think you could meet me at this address?"

"I could," Myles said. "But why?"

"Because a man of the cloth suggested you do so. Can you make it?"

"I can," Myles said. "I can."

"Very good," said O'Carroll. "That's excellent. I saw you were trying to get out the window before I got here?"

Myles blushed. "I was," Myles said. "I apologize. I wanted—"

"You know the latch is broken," said O'Carroll. "The workmen are fixing it tomorrow. That is, if you still want to use your singular method of exit."

To this, Myles had nothing to say. He wondered if this odd, kind, gentle man had sprung out of dreams he'd harbored since childhood, when he wished he had a priest neither stern nor forceful. A priest who was simply a guiding hand. Myles feared he might be asleep or—perhaps more likely—a victim of the Woodrat's paint fumes.

"I would say, 'I hope to see you,' but that makes no sense," O'Carroll said. "I know I'm going to see you."

CHAPTER EIGHT

Around three the next day, Myles set out from his tenement apartment and walked the many blocks up to 8th Street. On the way, he passed by Grantly's, a drugstore that sold his favorite hair cream, and Migni's, a grocery store that stocked all sorts of exotic fruits. Alberto Migni sold kumquats, kiwis, and avocados, as well as a few other fruits that sounded even more imaginary.

On the rare day when Myles journeyed this

far uptown, he had trouble keeping himself from browsing the selection at both places. On this particular day, however, Myles couldn't make it to 8th Street fast enough. The kindly O'Carroll struck him as a man who could save his life. Just thinking about Carly made pain shoot through his chest.

Myles dreamt of the kinds of things O'Carroll might have to give him. He thought of a special oil or a secret, pain-relieving drink. He envisioned a magical eucalyptus tree, the kind Myles had heard they grew in Australia. Whatever O'Carroll gave him, the fact that a priest had appeared in his life at all meant that somehow, the Lord had blessed him.

He searched for the address on the east side when he made it to 1st Avenue. Near a streetlight next to a barbershop, a horse trader sold saddles at a discount. Walking by the horse trader, Myles counted from twenty-two upwards until he got to ninety-eight. He found a small wooden door marked by a carving of a harp. He went down three small steps and knocked on the door. No answer.

Myles knocked again. A man no more than five feet tall yanked it open and looked up suspiciously.

"What do you want?" he said. "You notice I didn't answer the first time."

"I'm looking for Father O'Carroll," Myles said.

"Father?" the man said. "Oh, right. O'Carroll. He's coming at four. You can wait here. It's quarter till."

"I appreciate the hospitality, sir," Myles said. He nodded and bowed his head in hopes of putting the short man at ease.

"I never said you could wait inside," the man said. "Like I said, Patrick comes at four. Wait here."

Myles stepped back as the man shut the door in his face. He crossed his arms. Was it possible the whole thing was a trick? Could it be that O'Carroll enjoyed playing pranks on kids who didn't know any better? It was too cruel to contemplate, but if it were true, it meant O'Carroll was like the priests Myles knew growing up. They didn't enjoy pranks, but they did enjoy teaching boys a lesson, especially with the help of a paddle or a thorny switch.

O'Carroll ambled down the street a few minutes later. Spotting Myles, he clapped his hands. He gave Myles a pinch on the back of his neck and gruffly shook his hand.

"Good to see you," he said. "I promise you're doing the right thing." After knocking on the door, rappity-rappity, the short man again came calling.

"Good to see you, Father," he said, a grin breaking out as he nodded at O'Carroll. "What ails you on this?"

"*Porto sancto*," O'Carroll said.

"*Ad porto sancto*," the man said. "Learn your grammar."

"*Ad porto sancto.*"

"Come in."

O'Carroll brought Myles into a basement apartment consisting of three small rooms. In each room, bookcases filled with trinkets lined the walls. In room number one, tin beer mugs, elegant harps, and jars of fresh soil covered the musty shelves. Labels on the jars listed the names of counties in Ireland. The second room boasted a tambourine, a harpsichord, and several violins. The final room included a table with three chairs.

The short man urged Myles and O'Carroll to sit down. Here, the bookshelves were stocked with locked chests. Myles noted that most of the chests were covered with complex swirls.

"It's Irish," Myles said. "Everything here is Irish."

"Correct," said O'Carroll.

"Here's how this works," said the short man. "I sell you something from my stores. At no point now or till the end of time do you ask me where it came from. At no point do you tell anyone that you came here. Am I clear?"

"I think he understands," said O'Carroll.

"Let the kid speak."

"I get it," Myles said.

"Glad to hear it," the short man said. He removed a chest with an engraving of a white cow above the keyhole. He fished through his pockets and pulled out a ring that must have held a hundred keys. After cycling through them, he opened the chest. Inside were three pieces of warped, tangled metal.

"Know what these are?" O'Carroll said to Myles.

"No," Myles said.

The short man picked up one of the metal pieces and cradled it gingerly in his palm.

"Trinkets?" Myles asked.

"Trinkets!" the short man said. "Ha. Very funny. These 'trinkets' are ancient relics."

"Ah."

"That's right," said O'Carroll. "Know them well. A man I know discovered all three in the soil near the monastery at Kells. Is Kells a familiar name to you, Myles?"

Myles remembered his visit to the place. He had been nine years old. Decked out in a brown robe, he'd kneeled on the stone floor of the sacred monastery and prayed for the safety of his people.

"I know it, yes," he said.

"Then its import is clear." O'Carroll picked up the relic on the right of the chest. As he turned it in the light of the gas lamp, the relic's tarnished metal glinted, just barely. It was twisted in an elaborate knot, a shape familiar to Myles from his trips to the church. To him they always looked like snakes getting lost.

"If worn correctly, it works as a barrier," said O'Carroll. "Store it in your pocket for a full day before the fight begins. At some point in that day, make sure to pray three times. If you do all this, your opponent won't be able to hit your most vulnerable spot. Am I clear?"

Myles felt a tingly feeling radiate outward from his ribs. He thought of asking if the relic was working right then.

"Yes, I understand," he said. He reached out to take the trinket, but before he could grab it, O'Carroll closed his fist and pulled it away.

"Ah, ah, ah," he said. "My friend here cannot give out such valuable treasures on commission."

"Mouths to feed," the short man said.

"Twenty dollars," O'Carroll said. "I recognize the price is steep, but safety is a valuable commodity."

The muscles in Myles's face began to tighten and strain. Twenty dollars? He'd need to make three times what he normally won fighting to win that back. To earn enough money to bring over his family, he needed five times the average payout.

Was this the price of a blessing? He reached into his pocket and pulled out three weeks' earnings.

CHAPTER NINE

Like half the people Myles knew in New York, he had trouble finding time in his day to make true friends. When he wasn't scrounging for money, he was searching Lower Manhattan for decent work, or else clearing the rats from his cramped, dusty apartment. Most of the storekeepers he knew refused to hire Irish, and those few that did never paid as well as the Woodrat. When Myles had time off, it seemed disrespectful, even sinful, to waste it having fun.

The free time Myles spent in the Wood-rat was a rare exception to the rule. As the club was sort of his workplace, Myles felt comfortable relaxing there. He justified it by telling himself that he was scoping the place out, even when all he was doing was chugging bottles of flat soda at a table. Even though some part of him knew he was lying—and even though that same part knew it made no sense—the sight of Oakley and Tracey reassured him that he was being responsible. Thinking of the money he made for them, he could manage to breathe easy.

Three days after he purchased O'Carroll's relic, Myles nursed a glass of chilled cider at a table with Eddie Leary. He thought of Eddie as an acquaintance, though he knew that Eddie likely saw Myles as more of a friend.

"It's a crying disgrace, I tell you," Eddie said. He was talking with Myles about a new law that punished citizens for loitering. "It's clear why they did it, you know that? These thugs want to keep us Irish from getting together in gangs."

"The police have real crimes to think

about," said Myles. "Do you think it might be in your head?"

"Not a chance," Eddie said. "How many people stand around in 'groups of six or more'? Why did they choose that number? It's Irishmen looking for jobs, I tell you. They want us off the streets."

At the bar, Tracey poured a beer for a customer with a spindly mustache. When Eddie said "the Irish," Tracey rolled his eyes.

"New laws," Eddie said. "No Irish in decent neighborhoods. No Irishmen looking for work. Soon enough. they bar us from entering the country. It's a war, Myles. But you know and I know that nobody is brave enough to fight back."

"What do you mean by *they*?" Myles asked. "These people are not like the English."

"They aren't, but they wish they were," Eddie said. "They want us out of their country."

Oakley traded slips of crumpled paper with a man in a suit by the door. The man offered Oakley a cigar, and Oakley tucked it away in his pocket. Were the slips of paper odds? Was the man in the suit a bookie? Perhaps he was simply a brewer giving Oakley a receipt. It was strange, or at least it seemed that way to Myles, that he let his life depend on men whose business practices were a mystery. Oakley sold drinks and hosted fights, but Myles wondered what other kinds of activities kept the Woodrat safely in the black.

"My brother says I'm crazy, but I'm not," Eddie said. "I'm just a man who refuses to live with his eyes closed."

"Fair enough," Myles said, hoping to change the subject. "Say, what do you know about the old pagan myths?"

"Pagan?"

"The old Irish myths," Myles said. "You know. Before Saint Patrick. In the days when Ireland had druids instead of priests."

"Can't say I think much about it," Eddie said. "Those were unholy times."

"I don't deny that," Myles said. "What I want to know is how much about them you learned."

"Not much," Eddie said. "I remember a teacher who told me they worshipped animals. 'Don't we now?' I said. Told her that her students felt the same way about dogs and sheep. But I can't say I heard much about anything else."

"What do you think they were like, at a guess?" Myles said. "Do you think they understood magic?"

"What's wrong with you?" Eddie said. "That stuff is balderdash, the talk of false idols. Now stop trying to bring up unholy subjects before you besmirch his name."

Eddie spat into a nearby tin pot. Myles stared at the table. Eddie was right. It was wrong to pry into ancient magics, but what else was Myles supposed to do?

At home, the relic lay on his nightstand, taking up space beside a statue of the Virgin Mary. Up until that moment, he'd figured O'Carroll's blessing marked the relic as holy, but now he wondered if its pattern was an insult to God. As a shiver ran through him, he vowed to stash the relic in his closet and repent.

CHAPTER TEN

That night, as he lay on his bed, Myles drafted a letter to his youngest sister back home. Every week, he wrote a letter to a different member of his family. Now it was Orla's turn to hear about his life in the States. Most weeks, the letter was easy, but this week he struggled to describe his thoughts and feelings to his sister. He hunched over a sheet of paper and tried to do them justice.

Orla my dear—

I write to you this evening with very exciting news. It seems that I may have the money I promised this week. On Monday, the bar at which I work is having a celebration, and if all goes well . . .

"A celebration?" Myles questioned aloud his words. In the rest of his letters, Myles left out exactly how he earned his money, writing only that he worked in a bar for men who made fun of his name. In the days leading up to the big fight, however, it seemed cruel to keep the threat to his life from his family. What if he died in the Woodrat? What if his injury forced him to go back home?

He imagined his mother weeping over his body, laid out on the floor of their home in a mummy's wrap of bandages. Even if the fight didn't kill him, the shame of hurting his mother would be too much for Myles to bear. He balled up the paper and tossed it in the box he kept in place of a trash can. Opening to a blank page in his notepad, he tried to start again.

Dear Orla—
How are you? I read in my last letter to Mum

that your dance teacher believves you have talent. I always thought so—I remember you skipping about the house like a Russian ballerina—and I must say your brother is pleased to get word that you want to pursue it. New York dancers are wonderful—not quite as exciting as Paris but wonderful regardless—and the halls they perform in are the biggest you've seen in your life—I swear just one could house a hundred families. Hope things are well and your cough is doing better . . .

Dancers? What if this letter was the last letter Myles ever wrote? He put the letter aside and opened to a new page in his notebook. This time, he went for honesty:

Orla—

I'm writing this time because I need to ask you a question. It's an odd one, to be sure, but I trust you, as a young and virtuous girl, to tell me the truth in your heart. A priest in the city has given me a trinket which he says could help me earn money. I need this money—Lord knows I do—but I worry the trinket may harbor unholy magics. If you were in my

place, what would you do? Will the Almighty under-
stand how badly I need this help?

"Could help me earn money." Dishonest.

Instead of balling it up, Myles tore the letter in half, then shredded it into quarters and from there into eighths. He shoved the fragments of the letter off his bed and watched as they whirled to the ground. He got up and stepped over the clothing and trash on the floor of his cluttered apartment. He went through his front door and made his way to the stairwell. Outside, he sat on his stoop and rested his head in his hands.

Orla McReary. His baby sister. She was the only sibling he still thought of as a child. He looked up at the sky, surrounded by a ring of tenement rooftops, and wondered aloud what his sister deserved to hear. He expected no answers—nothing ever came to him the moment he asked the question—but he hoped that a prayer might sprout into a virtuous plan. Lowering his forehead to his knees, he clasped his hands together. All around him, neighbors talked, horses whinnied, and policemen chatted under streetlights. He raised his head and took in the dust and noise of the city.

———————

Upstairs, Myles sprawled on his bed. The ceiling of his apartment was covered in stains, the work of the person who'd lived there before him. He stared at a sooty black swirl until it appeared to move on the ceiling. He closed his eyes and hoped silently that the answer would arrive in a dream.

It came to him just before he drifted off for the night. When Myles was a boy, his father used to tell him about channeling, about getting faraway people to hold conversations with you by learning to write in their voice. The technique seemed mystical, like the relic itself, but if his father suggested it, Myles knew it had to be safe. Myles tore a new sheet of paper from his notepad and wrote in Orla's voice.

Myles—
I know it is very hard for you to make a hard choice like this but you are a good brother and I think

the Lord understands that. I think he knows what you do for us, and I think he knows you want to see your family, I know it must sound very strange to you but I believe in my heart that Father O'Hanlon knows what you do is a holy thing. Your sister loves you and Mummy and Daddy miss you and we read all your letters out loud over dinner every time they arrive in the mail. I had a tooth fall out the other day and Mummy told me if one more falls out she promises to knit me a new sweater and I want a new sweater because it has been very cold lately.

The point I am trying to make is I think you are doing the right thing and everybody misses you and Daddy says he is proud. Then again Daddy said he was proud when I lost my tooth so maybe it isn't very important what he said. I love you and I think you should keep doing what you are doing and stop feeling so sad about it all the time. Hope to hear from you soon.

—Orla

P.S. I don't know if I told you but Mummy and Daddy are teaching me how to cook and I made a nice mash the other day. It was tasty.

Myles read the words of the letter aloud in Orla's voice. He folded it in half and set it down on the table. Lying back on his bed, he looked again at the ceiling. This time, the swirling pattern didn't move, no matter how long he stared.

CHAPTER ELEVEN

On the day of the fight, Myles arrived at the Woodrat with less than an hour to spare. He fingered the relic in his pocket every few minutes on the walk from his apartment to the club. In line with O'Carroll's instructions, he'd kept it in his pocket for twenty-four hours, even sleeping on his side at one point so it didn't poke him through his pajamas.

When he got inside, he saw a massive crowd, speckled here and there with faces of people he knew. A few seconds after he stepped through the door, one of the onlookers peered over and pointed.

"Hey, boys! All hail the Scrawny One!" A loud, raucous cheer rang through the club, the kind of cheer that sounded a bit too much like a boo for Myles's comfort.

He waved. A disorderly man somewhere in the club hurled an empty pint glass at the wall. Even from the entrance, Myles could tell that Tracey was up to his eyeballs in work. Mayflower chewed on a sarsaparilla root and talked with a man in a bowler hat. Myles skirted around the crowd and found Oakley behind the bar.

"About time!" Oakley said. "Another half hour and I thought we might have a riot."

"Apologies," Myles said. "I got a big dinner to get ready." He was lying—it was hard to even finish the beef liver he'd bought from his butcher that evening.

"That's a good enough reason, I suppose," Oakley said. "How are you? I got you some cod liver oil if you need it to wake you up."

"I'm fine," Myles said, wishing he could run

out back and throw his guts up. "How's Carly?"

"Raring. I put him back in the storage closet to do whatever he does. There's a rumor he likes to rub butter on his chest."

"Butter?"

"To help deflect punches," Oakley said. "Speaking of which, if you want to try it, I've got this bucket of bacon grease."

"Really?"

"No!" Oakley said. "Myley, you can't be this gullible. It gets me worried sometimes."

In front of the bar, the crowd of spectators split into two factions. The factions gathered on two opposing sides of the floor. One side included the men Myles knew. The other side consisted of all strangers.

"What's going on?"

"Uptown versus downtown," Oakley said. "The Bowery versus Harlem. Keep an eye out for jokers flinging bottles."

Myles stood on tiptoe and peered around the room. "No bottles," he said.

It was hard not to notice the differences between the two sides. Men from the uptown group wore sawdust-covered suits and finely trimmed mustaches. They stretched their blazers as their fists pumped in the air. The men from downtown had full beards and dowdy clothes. One man was so disheveled Myles wondered if he was homeless.

The downtown faction included Eddie. That was good. There were men in the crowd Myles hadn't seen in months. Ted Fiorello was cheering for Myles, in spite of the fact that Carly was Italian, like him. Myles felt warmth for these men, who had chosen to put their money on him in spite of Carly's unblemished record. He wanted to thank Ted and Eddie and John Barings Brown and Willington Kepler and Hermann and—

Father O'Carroll. By a wall near the downtown men, the father was talking with a man with bad acne. His collar was off, and he was dressed in black shoes; black dress pants; and a sharp, clean blazer. Myles tapped Oakley on the shoulder.

"Who's that?"

"Who's what?" Oakley said.

"That man." He pointed to the man with bad acne.

"Not sure," Oakley said. "But he's in a bad way. That man he's talking with is a scoundrel. I told him over and over to keep his mug on the streets."

"You kicked a priest out of your club?" Myles asked

"A priest?" Oakley said. "Arnie Wilkins, a priest. That's a laugh. That guy is the biggest con man this side of Broadway. I saw him try to sell the Hudson River to a pair of deaf kids from Boston. He doesn't get me, because I can see through him. But I hate when a man like that takes money from honest customers."

Myles felt his chest burn. "I thought that man was a priest."

"Lord, is that what he told you? I guess we do need to work on your gullibility. Last news I heard he was selling baldness cures from a wagon on Staten Island."

Myles clung to the bar. The whoops of the crowd turned slowly into jeers. He struggled not to pitch over and vomit.

"All that matters for us is that you stay away," Oakley said. "I've seen good men waste all their money on malarkey from people like him."

CHAPTER TWELVE

Oakley sent Myles to an empty storage closet so Myles could prepare for the fight. Myles followed in silence. When the door shut safely behind him, he stomped his feet in anger and hurled the relic against the wall. He'd treated a slimy huckster like a genuine man of the cloth. How could he be so stupid?

He thought of Father O'Hanlon, all the way back home. The man would've listed, in painful detail, all the sins that Myles had committed.

Worshipping false idols. Looking outside the church for supernatural guidance. Treating a dyed-in-the-wool sinner as he would treat Father O'Hanlon himself. Buying smuggled goods, which Myles figured was stealing.

His chest was wracked with pain. Oakley had left him a glass of water, and Myles downed it, glugging the murky liquid as though he'd spent the last week stranded on a raft. He conjured up images of his mother, his da, his siblings, his friends, his teachers, his neighbors, and his girlfriends. He had let these good people down. Myles wasn't a fighter, at least not a real one. Now a man who was born and bred for boxing was about to reveal him as a fool.

Myles hated how easily O'Carroll had tricked him. But he felt more foolish for tying up his future with a sport as savage as boxing. It was not even much of a sport at all. It was simply what people had been doing to each other from the very beginning of time. Myles was no better than the bullies he knew, those boys who threw nicer and weaker kids to the ground because it made them feel stronger.

He remembered his father telling him stories about the great Irish fighters when Myles was young. Cú Chulainn. Grace O'Malley. Eoin, the boxer of Kerry. His father said Eoin trained every day, getting ready for matches by throwing his fists into haystacks and running for miles. Eoin did this to protect his poor little town from highway robbers and bandits. A year after Eoin married his wife, she died at the hands of a vagabond. From that day forward, the fighter kept a lock of her hair in a necklace that he wore as a charm.

Wait a minute.

If a local hero in Kerry kept a charm inside a necklace, what was so different about Myles and his so-called relic? The relic was fake, of course. But the urge Myles felt to protect his family was all too real. What was so wrong about taking no chances to ensure that he survived his fight? It must be a good thing if he did it for the welfare of others, even if boxing itself was not a very good thing to do. As the Bible said, a thief is not a thief if he steals bread to feed his children. The McRearys were hungry. Why shouldn't Myles be forgiven?

The relic lay in the corner of a shelf. Myles reached in and picked it up. Arnie Wilkins had probably just grabbed a piece of junk left on the roadside. But in a way, the trinket's twisted metal looked beautiful to Myles because of what it meant. It proved once and for all that Myles was not a sinner. The words of his sister were right. He was simply doing his best to serve the people who had cared for him. He was serving the people who taught him the word of the Lord.

Out on the floor, the spectators called for Myles to come out and fight. He tucked the relic in his pocket. Flexing his arms, he hopped up and down and wrung out his hands. He crossed himself and stepped through the door.

CHAPTER THIRTEEN

"Prepare to meet your maker, scrawny!"

"Give 'im one for the Emerald Isle!"

"Don't let me down, Carly! I got twenty bucks on this!"

"What, are you sweating? The heat too much for you to bear?"

"The eyes! Always get the eyes!"

Inside the fighter's circle, Carly ground his fists together and hopped on the balls of his feet. Myles looked him over. Two scars marked the Italian, the one around his torso and another that formed a ceiling above his stomach. Both of the man's arms had enormous, bulging veins. For the first time, Myles felt he could look at Carly the way he looked of his other opponents—as a man he had the power to knock down, plain and simple.

For his part, Carly looked down at Myles's legs, then at his face, then finally at his stomach. An ache ran through Myles, running up from his ribs and spreading across his torso. He puffed out his chest and rubbed his hands together. The downtown crowd egged them on.

Oakley stepped into the space between the two crowds. He opened his palm and extended his hand to Carly, then to Myles, as though it was only this gesture that kept them from attacking each other. He clapped his hands.

"Gentlemen! Some of you have come very far to see this evening's match. I want to thank our friends up in Harlem for donating their star for this occasion."

The uptown crowd booed. "Donate?" one man yelled out. "What the heck does that mean?"

"It means that a certain barkeeper struck a deal with yours truly," Oakley said. "Point is, today we are gathered for the best fight in Manhattan history. Judging from the bets you fine men put down, I expect this to be a match to remember."

He glanced at Myles and winked. "Are you ready?"

"I'm ready," Myles said.

"He's ready!" yelled the downtown crowd.

"Monsieur Sperio, you ready?" Oakley said.

"As always," Carly said.

"It's settled," Oakley said. "You know the rules, boys. Fight!"

At the bar, Tracey rang a bell. Carly hunched over and put up his dukes. Myles stood tall and turned to his side, guarding his chest with his right fist. Carly and Myles circled each other on the floor. Carly lunged, barely swiping Myles on the left cheek with his knuckles. Myles feinted, jerked back, and socked Carly in the armpit. He tried to move closer and land a stronger punch.

Carly was fast, though. His legs moved sideways so quickly Myles wondered if the Italian was hovering off the ground. Myles leapt backward, positioning his right fist for a sidewinder. Carly came forward, and Myles popped him in the nose. Carly staggered back and nearly fell.

"Look at that! Good Lord!"

"He's bleeding!"

"I told you eejits never to bet against the Irish!"

Droplets of blood fell down from Carly's nose. They mixed with the sweat on his chest and spread across him in veinlike trickles. Myles felt the knuckles on his right hand go numb. When he rubbed them and cradled them in his left palm, Carly rushed forward and smacked him on the cheek.

"There we go! One to one! Now this is a fight!"

"Sicilians eat scoundrels like you for dinner!"

"Get up! Get back up, you dog!"

Myles propped himself up on his elbow. He scrambled back up and dodged a second blow from Carly. His vision was blurry now, and when he looked at Carly, he saw a black mass where sweat-covered hair should have been.

Myles ran forward and swung again. Carly ducked away and crab walked to the right. Myles flailed, swinging his pained arms in front of him like a blind man, until finally his fist landed on Carly's left shoulder. For a second, Myles felt satisfied, but then Carly spun and pounded Myles in the ribs. Myles crumpled and fell to the ground.

CHAPTER FOURTEEN

Myles's vision filled up with dots and pulsing red figures. Pain shot up from his ribs. He tried to push himself up on his feet, but his muscles refused to move. His weak bones shook like broken bells in his chest.

"That's it. That's the end."

"Downtown fighters are weak, I tell you."

"Graces. That child looks awful."

"How many bottom feeders just lost half their salaries?"

Carly shot Myles a wolfish stare. On the end

of the downtown side, Oakley watched Myles with the clinical eye of a doctor.

This is it, Myles thought. *I'm a cripple from this day forward.*

He crawled on his elbows over a small patch of floor. The relic pressed on his skin through the fabric of his shorts.

What did it mean to be a warrior, he wondered. Did it mean you were someone who won? Did it mean you knocked your opponents down every time with overwhelming strength? Or did it mean that you fought through the pain? That you struggled to victory no matter the cost to your body?

It wasn't glamorous to keep going until you collapsed, but it was honorable. Myles had the sense that it was better to go out with dignity than to give up on the future of your family just to save your own skin.

He thought back to the sight of his father standing up to their landlord. He saw the rain and the wind beating down, the landlord huddled in his big winter coat while his father told him to leave.

Myles rolled onto his stomach and coughed. He placed his hands in a push-up position and forced himself up off the ground. At that moment, Carly grabbed him by the waist and began to choke him in a vise grip. Myles twirled and wrenched his arm around Carly's unguarded neck. The two locked together in a fierce standing grapple, each fighter spreading his legs apart to maintain balance on the floor. Hoping to pry off Carly's hands, Myles put his weight into his shoulder.

Carly loosened his grip. Myles realized what the man was doing—getting ready to jump back so Myles would hurl himself onto the ground. Sure enough, Carly pushed forward suddenly and backtracked away from Myles. Myles let go too, hopping to stay on his feet.

Sweat and blood stung Myles's eyes. He pressed them with the palms of his dirty hands. He stared at Carly, the two unmoving in the din of the shrieking crowd.

"What's wrong, Carly? Scared of a boy from the slums?"

"Show him what Sicily is made of!"

"Catholic showdowns, I tell you. Can't beat 'em."

"Get him now!"

Before Carly could move, before Myles even knew what he was doing, Myles hit Carly with a sudden, brutal uppercut. It landed beneath Carly's chin and let out a terrible crack. Carly went down, unconscious, and the downtown crowd exploded into cheers.

CHAPTER FIFTEEN

After the fight, Oakley counted up the incredible earnings from the evening. In the wake of the match, the downtown spectators treated Myles like a king, lifting him up above the crowd and chanting his name throughout the club. Myles, who disliked celebrations, thought the whole thing was confusing and scary. In the back room, alone with Oakley, he gradually came back to his senses.

"Unbelievable," Oakley said. The fight had

made them so much money that Oakley could only store a third of it in the chest where he stored their earnings. He piled the rest—minus Lew Mayflower's cut—in a crate, which Oakley kept hidden from the rest of the bar underneath a thick black curtain.

"Look at this, kid. You're rich. We all are. With this kind of money you could move into a place on Wall Street."

Myles waited silently for his payout.

"I mean it," Oakley said. "A wonderful show. You could step out of the ring right now and do something incredible with your life. Start a business. Write a book. Whatever you want."

"I suppose."

Oakley counted up Myles's share of the profits. Ten dollars. Twenty dollars. Thirty. When he counted up forty dollars, Myles felt a lump in his throat. When Oakley counted to fifty, Myles's heart began burning. This kind of money was beyond his position, beyond his class. Could it really be possible that the money was his? Quietly, Myles imagined a banker or a politician swooping in and telling him sorry, there's a problem, these earnings belong to us. Yet nobody knocked on the door.

"Here you go," Oakley said. "A hundred and ten."

"You're joking."

"No joke. Imagine what I can do with this place with all these profits. I can't wait to show them to Mr. Mayflower. I'm thinking Versailles or maybe a Buckingham on the Bowery. Either way, expect renovations."

"Versailles?" Myles said."

"It's a gag!" Oakley said. "We should work on your sense of humor on top of that gullibility. It's a drag when a bright kid like you doesn't know how to take a joke."

"I'm sorry."

"Don't be sorry. Be happy. Go home and buy yourself whatever you think you deserve. You've earned it."

Myles cradled the hundred and ten dollars in his hand. He removed a bill and held it under the light. It was real. It was not a counterfeit. The money was his. Myles thanked

Oakley and slipped out the club through the back door. As he left the Woodrat, hollers leaked through the front door and followed him down the street.

CHAPTER SIXTEEN

The next day, after waking up early, Myles went to a fancy restaurant and ate a fancy breakfast. He ordered expensive bacon, fine tea, good coffee, and well-cooked eggs. He ate his food slowly in a room full of high-flying patrons.

Myles ate alone. As he did, he kept his hands off the clean white tablecloth, afraid he might stain them with dirt or grime from his apartment. The waiter kept his distance, and Myles worried that perhaps he smelled bad. He made a mental list of the tasks ahead as he slowly devoured his meal.

The first thing was to go to the bank and transfer funds overseas. The second was to write a letter telling his family where to pick up the money. The third was to get a decent haircut and shave, preferably at the barber on 11th Street, followed by a trip to the spa for a nice bath. Then a tailor, for decent clothes.

When he wrote the letter, the jubilant tone he felt it needed somehow felt unnatural. He looked forward to his family arriving on the boat, and yet he knew how difficult it might be for his father to get a job. Likewise, his mother would have to work to keep their family in a decent apartment. There weren't many neighborhoods Irish people could move to, but even so, Myles made a pledge to find his family a respectable space before they came. He'd proved to them yesterday that he could make good, and now he needed to prove that he could live decently.

After paying the bill, he made his way down to the bank. He filed the wire transfer and tucked the receipt in his pocket. Outside, the day was sunny. The light's reflection on the East River nearly blinded him. He went to the post office and slowly wrote the letter to his family. When he finished, he dropped it in the mailbox, then regretted it instantly, wishing it were possible to take it back and look over it one more time.

A dock stood next to the post office. Myles went out to an empty pier. After taking off his shoes, he dipped his feet in the New York water for the first time since he arrived. Steamships and barges rolled by on the filthy waves. Pigeons and seagulls cawed and flew over his head. When Myles felt something on his leg, he lifted it out of the water. A strand of seaweed clung to his ankles.

He took the trinket out of his pocket. While dressing that morning, he put it there unconsciously, as though he expected to fight for his life once again. Myles turned it around several times and winced as the tarnished metal sent harsh sunlight toward his eyes. In the distance, a factory in Jersey belched plumes of smoke into the air.

Would Myles stop fighting? His mother wouldn't want him to box, but if he made this kind of money, his father might try to change her mind. Moral rightness was hard to uphold in the face of a hundred dollars.

Myles got up and pulled on his shoes. His wet toes squelched in his socks. Holding up the trinket, he looked at it one last time. A whistle went off in the distance. Myles threw the trinket into the river, where it skipped off the surface, once, twice, three times. It broke through the surface and sunk into the water. Myles turned away and headed back to the club.

ABOUT THE AUTHOR

A. S. Acheson is a writer and a graduate student at Trinity College, Dublin.

WELCOME TO

THE DOJO

BODY SHOT
PATRICK JONES

HEAD KICK
PATRICK JONES

SIDE CONTROL
PATRICK JONES

TRIANGLE CHOKE
PATRICK JONES

LEARN TO FIGHT,
LEARN TO LIVE,
AND LEARN
TO FIGHT
FOR YOUR
LIFE.

AFTER THE DUST SETTLED

The world is over.
Can you survive what's next?

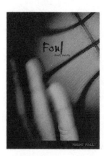